KU-229-398

Thanks to the Rural History Centre,
University of Reading

3

A Catalogue record for this book is available from the
British Library.

ISBN 0 340 72712 8

Printed and bound in Great Britain by Guernsey Press,
Guernsey, Channel Islands

Hodder Children's Books
A division of Hodder Headline plc
338 Euston Road
London NW1 3BH

This . . .

is Eddie Crabtree.

Eddie is an ordinary boy, living in an ordinary town, doing ordinary things. But Eddie has some extraordinary ancestors.

Like Diggory Crabtree, Eddie's Victorian
ancestor . . .

This is Diggory's story . . .

1

Mrs Evadne D'Abney, founder and secretary of the Society for the Improvement of the Deserving Poor, was finding it hard to conceal her disappointment. She had given over her large and elegant drawing room to this month's meeting of the Society, but as things turned out, she could have held it without discomfort to anybody in a hackney cab. There were five persons present; herself, her husband Josiah, the two Miss Etons, spinsters of Mrs

D'Abney's acquaintance, and Josiah's business partner, Mr Poole. And now it seemed that Mr Poole was having second thoughts.

"I really see little point in the Society's continuing!" he grumbled. "There is clearly no interest in improving the lot of the poor, deserving or otherwise. You ought to shut up shop, Mrs D'Abney, and save yourself further embarrassment."

"But Mr Poole!" cried Mrs D'Abney. "Our work is surely too important to abandon. As Josiah has said—"

"Forgive my bluntness," Mr Poole interrupted. "I like Josiah. Like him enormously. But he's a soft-hearted fool. I don't think I ever met a deserving beggar, and I dare swear I never will.

Most of the poor, it seems to me, are poor because they can't be bothered to better themselves. Educating them isn't going to change their nature, which is bone idle. I've gone along with this nonsense so far for Josiah's sake, but now I think it's time to make my excuses and go."

Mr Poole stood and strode to the door. At the last moment he turned. "It's your money Josiah. How you waste it is your affair. But if you ask me, this thing has been a fool's errand from the start!" And with that, he nodded to the founders of the Society, and left.

The silence that followed his parting was finally broken by the younger of the two Miss Etons.

"Dear Mr Poole," she trilled, "Always so
. . . er . . . forthright in his views!"

"I believe I smelled spirits on his
breath," the elder Miss Eton said, and she
shuddered slightly.

"The poor man hasn't been the same
since his wife passed away," said Josiah.
"His dear mother is quite beside herself
with worry over him."

"Still," Mrs D'Abney said in a
wounded tone. "I had hoped that a man
like him, who has risen from poor
beginnings himself, might have had a
little more sympathy for the poor. And . . .
well . . . I had been hoping that he might
have donated some of his wealth . . . Oh,
what are we to do, Josiah?"

"Perhaps, my dear," her brother said
after a few moments thought, "perhaps
our little society would attract more
attention if we could hold up an example
– a prototype, if you will – to demonstrate
what a difference an improving influence

could make to the rough clay of the common person?"

"A prototype! Of course!" Mrs D'Abney leapt from her chair, and began to circle the room like a clockwork toy. "Find a suitable young person – poor, but with potential – teach him, train him, shape him . . . and then present him to the world, improved and polished. People would have to take notice. As usual, dearest, you have struck the nail squarely upon its head! But who to improve?"

"What about one of our own servants?" Josiah suggested.

"Our own servants?" Mrs D'Abney looked at him in surprise. "Oh my dear, if we did that, who would run the household? No no, it must be an outsider. I shall begin my search tomorrow."

2

"She'm lookin' at you, Digg."

"Oo is?"

"That posh awld biddy with the
squire. She'm lookin' at you.
You dun summut wrong Digg?"

"No."

"Then why's her lookin' at you?"

"She ent!"

"She is."

"She ent. Now shut up and waggle yer rattle. They crows is back."

Diggory Crabtree and his friend Sam Daskett were working partners. They worked twelve hours a day, seven days a week, pacing the fields of the squire's farm, waving rattles. It kept the birds off the newly planted seeds, and it earned them 3 ½d per day.

"My dad seen the squire's new steam tractor Yesserdy." Sam announced, "You seen it, Digg?"

"Not close up, but I seen it. Brilliant, it is. So clever – the way they takes a bit o' water, and makes it—"

"Brilliant? Clever?" Sam was horrified. "Them new-fangled machines is goin' to be the death of farmin', my dad sez!"

"Don't stop 'em bein' clever though, do it?" Diggory said quietly.

They worked for a while in silence –

well – relative silence. But as they came back up the field, Sam said. "She'm still there. She'm still lookin at you. You sure you ammt dun nuthin'?"

" 'Course I'm sure. Same's I'm sure she ent lookin' at me. What would a posh biddy like her want with the likes of me, anyroad?"

At that moment, Diggory spotted a flurry of crows landing at the far end of the field. He set off, whooping and rattling, and Sam set off after him. So they both forgot the lady with the squire.

But Sam was right. The lady *had* been watching Diggory, as he found out when he arrived back home that evening. There, sitting at the only table in the only room of the tiny cottage was the "awld biddy". And standing behind

her was the squire himself. Diggory stood there, uncertain what to do, until he felt his hat being snatched off.

"Show some respect for yer betters," his dad growled.

"I've been speaking with your Mater and Pater, Diggory," the squire said.

"Oo?" Diggory asked.

"Us!" his dad muttered.

"And it's been agreed," the squire continued. "Mrs D'Abney here is taking you to London."

London??! Diggory was stunned. London?! The squire kept talking, explaining all about Mrs D'Abney's Society and what it planned to do, but Diggory wasn't listening. One thought kept going round and round in his head.

The Smoke, they called it. The Big City. Sam's dad had been there once, to see the meat market at Smithfield and he'd sworn never to go back there as long as he lived. London had everything, Mr Dackett said – cholera, crime, poverty, pick-pockets, stinking fog, gaudy women and tawdry men.

Mind you, Diggory thought, Martha was in service there, and she seemed happy enough. Martha was Diggory's eldest sister. She worked below-stairs in a posh London house.

Hey, thought Diggory suddenly, if I go to London, I could look her up. We could go to a Magic Lantern show together – ride in a cab to Buckingham Palace, see the queen . . . Maybe London wouldn't be so bad after all . . .

"Diggory?" Diggory snapped out of his daydream. The posh biddy was talking.

"Yes 'Mmm?"

"Mrs D'Abney was explaining," said the squire, "how her Society will work for you."

"It's rather like a gardener, Diggory," the lady said, glancing around the overcrowded room, "taking a young plant from a . . . um . . . rather harsh environment, and bringing it into the greenhouse, where it may be protected and nurtured."

" 'N'orchard?" Diggory exclaimed. "You told I, I were gonna live in a greenhouse!"

The squire stepped in at this point, explaining things to Diggory in a more straightforward way.

"So," said the boy when the squire was done, "I'm to live with you, am I, M'm? In a posh 'ouse in London? What, with servants an' that?"

Mrs D'Abney nodded. "With hard work Diggory," she declared, "at the end

22

of your time with us, you will be in a position to considerably improve your lot!"

Diggory looked around the large family that had now gathered, mainly to gawp at Mrs D'Abney. "What? This lot?"

"No Diggory," Mrs D'Abney said, "Your lot! Your chance in life. The future is coming, Diggory, and we at the Society for the Improvement of the Deserving Poor are here to help you make the most of it!"

3

Two weeks later, Diggory Crabtree found himself sitting aboard one of the latest steam locomotives, hurtling towards London at a staggering, heartstopping fifty miles per hour.

He had never been on a train before, let alone in the padded luxury of a first class carriage like this one. He should have been enjoying the ride, luxuriating in the softness of his seat, but a number of things were spoiling the journey for him.

First of all there was the new suit. Mrs D'Abney herself had bought it, and had it sent from some posh shop in Town. The squire's own footman had brought the box round to the cottage. The whole family had gathered round to watch as Diggory had torn off the wrapping and lifted the lid . . .

His brothers and sisters had giggled,
Even his father had smirked. A sailorsuit!

"Do she live on a island then, Digg?"
his brother had asked — just before he
collapsed into fits of
laughter. And the
humiliation hadn't
ended there. This
morning, on the
carriage ride to the
station, they had
been followed all the
way by the howling
laughter of the
village children.

Dressed in the
suit, Diggory
looked ridiculous.
It didn't feel very
comfortable either.
Whether it was
the cloth or the bath he'd been forced
to have he did not know, but something

was making Diggory's legs itch like mad. The shoes were agony too. All the shoes he had worn in the past had been hand-me-downs, thoroughly broken in by four older brothers. These were brand new and hard as iron. It was like wearing boilers with boot-laces.

But painful and embarrassing though the new clothes were, they were not what was irritating Diggory most. What was irritating Diggory most was sitting in the seat opposite. William D'Abney was everything Diggory had imagined a la-di-da rich boy would be – scrubbed up, dressed up . . . and stuck-up. Mrs D'Abney had brought him along, so that he and Diggory could "get to know one another". But all William did for the first part of the journey was read his book. Diggory had only held one book in his life. That was the hymn-book at church, and he couldn't read that – he'd just pick it up when he needed something to hit Sam with.

After half an hour, the rattle and
bump of the train sent Mrs D'Abney off
into a light sleep. Finally, William looked
up from his book. He looked Diggory
slowly up and down, taking note of the
country boy's red, work-worn hands and
sunburnt nose.

"So," he said, looking down his own
nose, "You're the common little urchin
who's coming to stay with us."

"I ent common," said Diggory
defiantly. "There's only one of I!"

"One of me – not one of I," William

corrected, "If you're staying with gentlefolk, you might at least learn to speak properly."

"Ent nuthin' wrong with the way I speaks. I ent never had no complaints afore!"

William tutted, shook his head, and went back to his book.

Diggory decided to take his mind of this nasty little toff. Reaching deep into his pocket, he drew out a brand new clay pipe. He was about to light it when he heard a little horrified gasp. Next instant, the pipe was snatched from his mouth.

SNICK.!!

"Wrrf -fff-y-gwwwwwwnnn?" Diggory spat

out the little bit of stem that was left clamped in his teeth, and repeated the question. "Wotchoo doing?"

"I should have thought that was obvious!" said Mrs D'Abney.

"Our dad gev us that! Thass a going-away present!"

"How appropriate then, that it's going away!" Diggory watched the pipe disappear into Mrs D'Abneys bag. "There will be no pipe-smoking while you are under my roof."

"But I always has a little pipe, of an evenin' – with me pint of beer."

"There will be no drinking of alcohol, either," Mrs D'Abney said, slightly shocked. "That will be your first improvement, Diggory."

No pipe. No beer. Diggory slumped back into the chair like a man condemned. He could see William smirking on the other side of the carriage, and spent the rest of the journey wondering how "improved" his

companion would look with a black
eye . . .

4

Diggory stepped off the train . . . and felt like Jack stepping off the beanstalk. The smoke and steam were like a land of clouds, out of which the station rose like a great palace of pillars and arches and glass. The only difference was that

in a palace, he wouldn't have been
jostled, and barged, and very nearly run
over by luggage trolleys every two
minutes.

Mrs D'Abney's coach was waiting to meet them. The luggage was loaded, and the two boys were hustled inside. Then with a crack of the whip, the coach clattered out of the station . . . and straight into the rush-hour crush.

As they crawled and edged and manoeuvered through the congested traffic, Diggory stared open-mouthed at the bustle all around. They'd said in the old days that the streets of London were paved with gold. Right now you couldn't even see the pavements.
There were people
everywhere.

All the men looked tall in their top
hats, and all the women looked like hand-
bells, in their big dresses. There were
organ-grinders, and knife-grinders, and
stalls selling hot coffee and hot chestnuts
and hot potatoes.There were beggars and
peddlers and street urchins and peelers
and everyone looked orange in the light of
the street lamps. Diggory wondered how
they lit them. Did someone climb up with
a ladder, or did the organ grinder's
monkeys earn extra peanuts by shimmy-
ing up with matches . . ?

He was still wondering ten minutes
later when the coach stopped. A servant
in a blue striped waistcoat opened the
carriage door, and Diggory leapt down.
He was standing in front of an arch.
A big black metal arch, supported on
two black metal lions sitting on two
brick pillars. Hanging from the arch
was one of those gas lamps, which
lit the way to a flight of steps, which
led in turn to a huge, shiny, black,

35

panelled door. The door swung inwards, and there, holding it open, stood a uniformed man-servant.

"In you go, Diggory," Mrs D'Abney called. So in Diggory went.

"Woss this?" Diggory asked the servant. "The Tower o' London? Bukkenam Palliss?"

"This, bumpkin, is my home!" said William D'Abney.

A home? Diggory looked around in disbelief. This was someone's home? His parish church was smaller than this. Everywhere he looked he saw things his home didn't have – carpets, big windows, high ceilings with fancy plaster mouldings, oil lamps with unchipped chimneys, a fireplace in every room, and over every fireplace a marble mantelpiece with a clock on it. And most of all, the biggest, comfiest looking armchairs he'd ever seen, with those fancy napkins on the back to stop the gentlemen's hair-oil leaving a stain. A home fit for a king . . . a home, from now on, fit for Diggory Crabtree. He ran full tilt across the room, and with a whoop started bouncing on the armchair.

There was a squeak of alarm from Mrs D'Abney. "Diggory!" she cried, "a young man of breeding does not leap about on furniture like . . . like a mountain goat!" Diggory climbed down.

"Sorry Missis. I din't know."

"That," William hissed, "is because you are a bumpkin!"

Over the next few days, Diggory had to learn a great deal that was new to him. On his very first night, Mr D'Abney found Diggory wandering in the garden, "Lookin' for the privvy".

"My dear boy! The bathroom is in the house." Josiah told him. "That can't be 'ealthy, surely!" Diggory said.

And still there was more to learn.

He had to learn that: "One does not need to wipe one's feet on the way out of a house"; "One wipes one's nose on one's handkerchief, not one's sleeve,"; "One does not call the servants 'me ducks' or 'me darlin' ' or 'luv' or ' 'ere, mate' ".

"Now, Diggory," said Mrs D'Abney, after one of these early lessons, "Have you any questions?"

"Just one, missis . . .

Who's this bloke "Wunn" you keeps talkin' about?

Diggory's first full dinner with the family was a particular trial. The two Miss

Etons had been invited, so that they could see their potential "diamond" before he was polished; to observe him, so to speak, in the rough. Also invited was Mrs D'Abney's brother, Silas. Diggory ambled in and sat at table, but his jaw dropped at the sight of all the cutlery at his place. "What's all this ironmong'ry for?" he gasped.

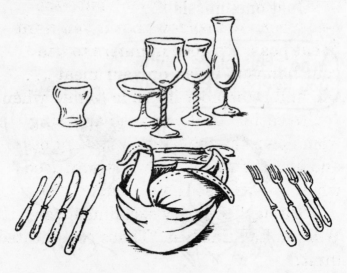

"Don't you have cutlery at your hovel?" William asked sweetly.

Diggory bristled. "Ye-ah." he said, "But

you don't need this lot for a bowl of soup an' a 'unk o' bread."

William thought for a moment, then turned with an angelic smile. "I'll explain," he said.

Diggory listened attentively, determined to impress.

"This knife," William whispered, "is for carrots only. The really big spoon in the bowl in the middle? That's the pea spoon. You borrow that if you want to eat peas. It's good manners to use your hands to break up your meat . . . Oh, and remember it's rude to talk when you're eating, so if you need anything from down the table, just reach across and get it. This fork here, is only used when . . ." And so it went on.

"Blimey!" Diggory exclaimed, when William had finished, "Thass complicated, innit?"

"You get used to it." William smiled. Then Josiah D'Abney said grace, and the meal began.

What with trying to remember "this
one for them . . . that one for these . . ."
Diggory was too busy to notice what the
others were doing, until he realised that
they weren't doing anything at all. He
looked up . . . to find the whole table had
stopped eating, and was watching him
in horror. He had a hunk of meat and a

fork in one hand, another fork tucked
behind his ear, while his free hand was
trying to cram a soup ladle full of peas
into his open mouth.

Mrs D'Abney patiently explained the
real purpose of the various pieces of
cutlery, and the dinner continued,
although for some reason, Diggory didn't

feel hungry any more.

Except for revenge, of course.

With the misery of dinner finally over,
Diggory looked forward to getting away
from William. But Mrs D'Abney had other
plans.

"Why don't you show Diggory the
playroom, William?" she said.

William was appalled. The playroom was
his special place – his holy of holies. Not even
his governess was allowed in, and yet he was
supposed to share his precious toys with this
. . . *street arab!* Mrs D'Abney, however, was
insistent, so William grudgingly led the way.
"There it is!" he said, flinging open a door.

Diggory stood in open-mouthed wonder. This toff had every toy he had ever dreamed about – and more!

There were bats and balls and tops and hoops and bugles and boats, and tin soldiers and puppets and even a Noah's Ark to play with on Sundays.

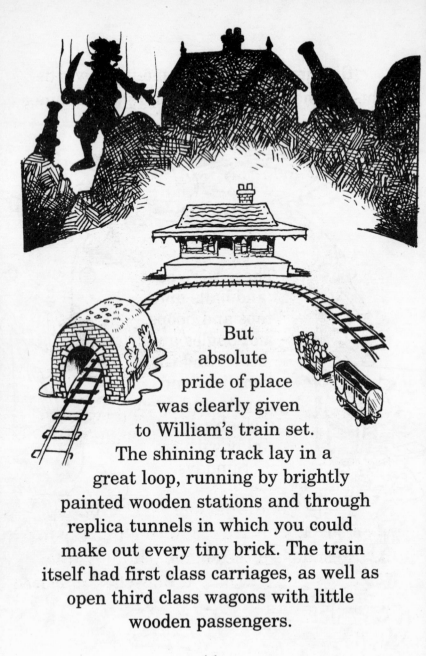

But
absolute
pride of place
was clearly given
to William's train set.
The shining track lay in a
great loop, running by brightly
painted wooden stations and through
replica tunnels in which you could
make out every tiny brick. The train
itself had first class carriages, as well as
open third class wagons with little
wooden passengers.

46

But the real star, for Diggory, was the locomotive. It sat on the rails, gleaming and irresistible like tin treasure, its clockwork key set in and ready.

Diggory fell to his knees, and began to wind it up. "Don't touch that!" William snapped.

"But your mam said . . ."

"Never mind what she said," William sneered. "It's my train and you aren't to touch it." He snatched the engine painfully from Diggory's grasp, wound it himself, and placed it on the tracks.

Nothing happened.

William wound again. Still the train sat there, Stubborn and unmoving.

"You've broken it!" William gasped.

"I ent!!"

"Uncle Siiii-laaaaaas!!"

Uncle Silas came bustling up the stairs. He was a jolly, chubby man, with the face of an ageing cherub. At dinner he'd been the only grown-up to tell William off over the cutlery episode. "bad form", he'd called it. Diggory liked Uncle Silas.

"Now then!" the old man said, waddling into the room, "What's the trouble?"

William jabbed an accusing finger at Diggory. "He broke my engine!"

"Oh? Let's have a little look-see, shall we?"

Dropping onto all fours, Silas deftly removed the casing of the engine, and, squinted into the workings. "Drat!" he

said, patting his waistcoat pocket, "I've
left my spectacles downstairs. I can't
quite see what's . . ."

Diggory looked over the
old man's shoulder.

"It's the worm drive," he said. "It's
slipped out of it's housing, and it's fouling
the spring."

"And how would you know, Bumpkin?" William sneered.

"By jingo, Wills. The lad's right!" Uncle Silas said, peering closer. He fiddled about with a tiny screwdriver, then replaced the train on the rail.

Whrrrrrrrrrrrr! The engine began to barrel happily round the track. Uncle Silas heaved himself off the floor and subsided into an armchair. "I see we have an engineer in our midst!" he said.

"What, him?" William guffawed. "Hardly!"

"I like machines." Diggory shrugged. "I like lookin' at 'ow they works. I 'elped mend the church clock last yer. Dunno 'bout no 'engineer', though."

"Clocks eh? Well you know, the great Brunel himself started off as a watch maker's assistant."

"Broonwho?" said Diggory

"Isambard Kingdom Brunel," Uncle Silas said solemnly. "A genius, my boy. He built the railway on which you travelled to London!"

"What? All by hisself?!"

"Well . . . no. He planned it though. Masterminded the whole thing. Genius!"

"Uncle Silas is an engineer," William said.

"You must come to my workshop, sometime, Diggory. Would you like that?"

"Oh, yeah!" cried Diggory, "How 'bout tomorrow?"

"Ah. Not tomorrow sadly," Uncle Silas said. "Tomorrow you go to school."

"SCHOOL!!?" Diggory was aghast. "No one said nuthin' about no school!"

"Nevertheless," the old man said, "that is where you are going tomorrow. Mrs D'Abney has enrolled you at William's school, so you'll be together. Won't that be jolly?"

Diggory and William looked at each other. "Jolly" was not the first word that came to mind.

The large red brick building looked grim
in the grey light of Monday morning. As
the two boys walked through the
forbidding gates, into the yard, Diggory
looked up at the sign. Gold lettering
against a black background reminded
him that he was entering . . .

The
Hazlett School
for the Sons of
Gentlefolk

William turned to him. "Don't say anything if you can help it." he commanded. "It's bad enough that Mama sends me to school with a bumpkin, but there's no need to let the whole school know it as well. I shall introduce you as my mute cousin."

"Moot? Thass a sort of a lizard, in't it?"

"Not 'newt', imbecile, 'mute'," said William. "It means incapable of speaking. Lord knows it's near enough the truth. I can barely understand that yokel gibberish of yours!"

Diggory's fuse was getting shorter and shorter. "Any minute now," he thought, "this toffee-nosed twerp is going in them bushes." This, as you will see, turned out to be a quite remarkable prediction.

A voice rang out. A clear, sharp, upper-crust voice. It came from a group of older boys who stood like a copse of trees in one corner of the schoolyard.

"Well well," the voice said, "If it isn't

D'Abney. My personal piggy bank!"

One of the trees detached itself from the group, and came striding, hands in pockets, towards William and Diggory. The others straggled along behind, as if attached to the leader by an invisible thread.

"I hope you have some pocket money, Dabbers, old man," the leader said as he arrived, towering over them. "Y'see, I find myself a little short of funds."

"B . . . b . . . but . . . I gave you money on Friday, Pennycroft." William's face was a sort of uncooked pastry colour, and there was a squeaky tremor in his voice.

The older boy shrugged. "Spent." he said simply.

"Scragg him, Penny!" cried a thin boy with a face full of pimples.

William leapt into a sort of "boxing stance" – chin sticking out in front, backside sticking out behind, fists held high in front of his face. He must have seen it on some poster.

Diggory couldn't watch. He shut his

eyes. By the time he
opened them again,
William had
gone, a nearby
bush had
sprouted a
pair of flailing
legs, and
Pennycroft's
lackeys were
scraping ill-gotten
pocket money off the floor.

Diggory went over to the bush, and
pulled William free.

"If them's your 'gentlefolk'," he said,
"I'd hate to see the ungentle sort!"

William pulled away from his rescuer,
"Why didn't you help?" he hissed. "Why
didn't you say something?"

"I'm a 'moot' – remember?" Diggory
said.

The trees had finally noticed Diggory.
"What have we here?" Pennycroft

sneered. "Another piggy-bank? Come here, little piggy!" With brutal delight, he and his gang moved in on their new victim.

That afternoon, William and Diggory had trouble sitting down. Hardly surprising after six strokes of the cane from Mr Hazlett. What was more surprising was that William had never been happier. Back in the playground, he had watched Diggory turn into a writhing, squirming slippery octopus.

Neither Pennycroft nor any of his cronies could get hold of him, and within a minute, they were all lying on the floor, tied in knots and groaning.

"Keep him away from me!" Pennycroft had sobbed as he hobbled away. "He should be in a cage. He's a wild animal!"

"No he's not." William had said, "He's my friend!"

Now, as they nursed their "war wounds" William turned to Diggory. "Where did you learn to do all that?" he asked.

"The farm." Diggory replied. "Shearin' time. Me'n Sam used to help catch the sheep. If you can get the better of a prize ewe, big streaks o' nuthin' like Pennycroft ent no problem."

William was silent for a while. Then he suddenly blurted out: "Will you teach me how to do it?"

"Will you let me play with your train?" Another pause.

"Right. Get yer coat off. 'Ere
beginneth your first lesson . . ."

6

Mrs D'Abney had insisted, as part of Diggory's "improvement", that as soon as he could write at all, he should write to his parents. So . . .

DEre Ma & Pa
Iy dTez ityer
aWi a Bezt
digg

dere Ma & Pa
I Dint like it ere
first off But iss
not sub bad no mor
the skool ent bad
I've evun mayd frenz
wiv WILLiam - supryse
supryse luv Diggery

Hazletts School
Kent

Dearest Mother & Farther,
~ This here's my second term at
Hazletts and old Hazlett says
as how I'm doing well. In the
~~Holly~~ holidays I been sevrel
times to see Williams Uncle
Silas. Every one thinks as how
he's soft in the hed, but he
eynt ~ he's just ~~got~~ big
clever ideals is all. Hes
~~tort tout~~ tau~~ght~~ me
loads about enjineering &
stuff Say ~~hullo to Sam~~
If you see him
        yore loving son
•
            Diggory

62

Hazletts School,
Kent.

Dearest Mother & Father

I cannot tell you how happy I
am that you allowed me to come here.
Of course I miss you terribly, but I
am learning so much! Silas — it seems
so impertinent to call him simply
"Silas", but he insists — well, Silas thinks
I have the makings of a first rate
engineer. William has proved a true
friend, and the D'Abreys are kind.

I am sorry to hear that Martha
has not written lately, but you
need not be alarmed I'm sure. From
what I have seen, servants here
in town are kept busy enough —
She has not the time for writing
that I have!

Your loving son

Digg.

7

By late November, Mrs D'Abney was thrilled. Her belief in Diggory's potential had been gloriously justified. Indeed, the change in the boy was so great, that one morning she announced to Josiah, "I believe a small experiment is called for."

"We shall be having guests for dinner this evening," she announced to the boys that Sunday. "Including a Mr Poole. Diggory you will sit opposite this distinguished gentleman and keep him entertained."

"Very well, Mrs D'Abney," said the new, improved Diggory Crabtree.

"Oh . . . just for this evening, Diggory, you may call me . . . er . . . 'Aunt'."

"I beg your pardon?" Diggory and William looked at each other in wonder.

"Yes. For this night – and this night alone, Diggory – I am your aunt. I shall explain why later."

"Why then, Aunt it shall be, Miss . . . I mean . . . Aunt!"

"And what shall I call you, Mama?" William asked, " 'Captain'? 'General'? 'Your Imperial Highness' . . ?"

"A simple 'Mama' will do, William," said Mrs D'Abney.

The table was laid, and most of the guests had arrived. Diggory squirmed in yet another new suit. Now they only awaited the arrival of Mr Poole.

"I predict that this evening will be a triumph," Mrs D'Abney declared.

Her husband was less sure. "I do hope you are right, my dear," he sighed. "But I must warn you that just recently, Poole has become even more moody than before."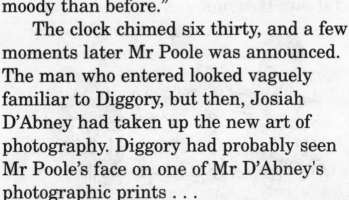

The clock chimed six thirty, and a few moments later Mr Poole was announced. The man who entered looked vaguely familiar to Diggory, but then, Josiah D'Abney had taken up the new art of photography. Diggory had probably seen Mr Poole's face on one of Mr D'Abney's photographic prints . . .

Dinner commenced. Diggory was determined to be a credit to his hostess. He spoke very nicely to his "aunt", and took every opportunity to draw Mr Poole into the conversation. He talked about the new steam ships, the recent war in the Crimea, the rumours Uncle Silas had told him that there would soon be electric lights, and wires that could carry the human voice. He talked and talked to Mr Poole, and Mr Poole replied so often with growls or grunts, that Diggory sometimes felt he was conversing with a bear.

It was during a discussion of mechanised farming that the disaster happened. Uncle Silas had been saying that, while the new steam ploughs were wonderful, it would be a pity if poor families suffered from the advance of machines.

"Who cares!" said Mr Poole suddenly, "There are plenty of jobs in the towns for those that want 'em, and if the idle can't be bothered to move to the towns, then let 'em starve. Country people have always been, at root, feckless and lazy!"

Diggory tried to bite his lip, but the

 words boiled up inside him. "I must disagree, Mr Poole," he said coolly. "My father and his colleagues on the squire's farm have never been shy of work. Indeed, considering their poor wages, I would say they go to it with remarkable willingness!"

"Your father?" Mr Poole's brow darkened, "his . . . his colleagues. But . . . I understood you to be . . ." He looked up the table towards Mrs D'Abney. The hostess smiled. The two Miss Etons tried in vain to suppress giggles.

"Mr Poole," said Mrs D'Abney, "allow me to present Diggory Crabtree. The first success of the Society for the Improvement of the Lot of the—"

She did not have time to finish. The smile was still fixed on her face when Mr Poole rose from his place like a human thundercloud. He turned on Mr D'Abney. "I don't appreciate being hoodwinked, Josiah!" he roared. The two Miss Etons shrank into their chairs. Mr Poole swayed slightly, but it did nothing to decrease his fearsomeness.

"Why, Mr Poole!" Mrs D'Abney protested, "Our intention was merely to demonstrate how—"

"Madam," Poole cut in. "I do not care a fig what you wished to demonstrate. I don't appreciate being made to  look a fool. Good evening to you all!"

A long and embarrassed silence followed his departure. It was finally broken by Josiah.

"I tried to warn you, my dear."

"Is it true that he mistreats his servants?" whispered the youngest Miss Eton. "One has heard . . . rumours."

A tiny bell sounded at the back of Diggory's mind. "Servants . . ." it went, "Servants . . . servants . . . SERVANTS!"

Suddenly Diggory remembered where he had seen Poole before. It was not in any photograph. His mind flashed back to the morning his sister Martha had left the farm to work, collected in a carriage by her new employers, a very old lady . . . and her son . . .

. . . Mr Poole.

"Diggory?" Mrs D'Abney said, as the boy leapt to his feet. "Where are you going? If you wish to leave the table you must ask to be excused. You know that! . . . Why

70

William! You too?! Come back this instant
. . . both of you. This instant! Do you hear
me?!"

Diggory arrived on the street just in

time to see Poole's
carriage disappear
around the corner.
Moments later William
cannoned into his
friends back.

"What was all that
about Digg? Why did you
run out like that?"

"Where does he live?"
Diggory demanded.

"Why Diggory –
you're crying! Can I
help?"

"Where does Poole
live William? Think!"
William gabbled an
address.

"How far?"

"Not far. It's by the
river."

"Come on."

They had no money for cabs or even the horse drawn omnibus, so they ran.

The gas lamps threw eerie shadows as the two friends reached Poole's neighbourhood. On one side of the road, they could hear the river lapping below the wall. On the other, a long row of fine houses stretched out until it disappeared into the murk. The two boys stopped, out of breath.

"Which is his house?" Diggory gasped, but William was too busy wheezing to even speak.

A group of ragged and filthy children were huddled by the river steps, sorting through a muddy pile.

Diggory pointed. "Let's ask them," he said.

"Them?!" William exclaimed. "But they're mudlarks!"

"So what?"

"Diggory. They pick stuff out of the river filth and sell it. They smell, Diggory!"

"Yeah! But this is their patch, and I'll lay odds there's not much they don't know!"

At that moment, one of the mudlarks glanced up. " 'Ere, look!" he called. "A couple of toffs!"

"Ne'er mind Toffs," Diggory said. Shrugging off his fancy accent he gave them Poole's name. They looked at each other. Obviously Poole had a reputation – and it wasn't for good works.

"Woss the trouble, mate," the oldest mudlark asked.

Diggory managed to say "my sister," before his voice choked up. But it was all the gang needed to hear. Leaving the smallest behind to guard their spoils, they led the two boys along the street. They found the house, and led Diggory to the basement steps.

"Come on," Diggory whispered.

"Not us!" said the mudlarks. "If the peelers caught us, we'd be in the Clink in a trice, for breakin' an 'entering."

"Oh, don't worry about that," William said. "My papa's a magistrate!"

"Well . . . all right. We're in!"

William and Diggory led the creeping band down the steps. "Is he?" Diggory murmured.

"Hmmm?"

"Your father. Is he a magistrate?"

"Er . . . no. But I thought we could do with some reinforcements."

"William!!"

Peering through a tiny window at the bottom of the steps, Diggory could make out two hazy figures. He took a deep breath, and tapped on the window. A moment later, the door was opened by a young man in servants livery. His wrist was bandaged.

He looked down at the two boys in their
full dinner dress, and
the ragged band of
mudlarks crowded
in the stairwell
behind them.
"Lawks,"
he said.

Diggory came straight to the point.
"I'm looking for my sister!" he blurted.

A girl's voice came from inside the room. "Who's that then, Bennet?" she asked. "Early carol singers?"

"Martha?" Diggory called. There was a pause. Then the girl's voice came again, much softer this time.

"Digg?"

Seconds later, Diggory was in grave danger of suffocation, as Martha Crabtree clutched him to her, and hugged him. She dragged him into the room "to get a good look at him". The valet, Bennet, tried to keep the others outside, but they piled in behind Diggory, an unstoppable wave.

Last time Martha had seen Diggory he hadn't even had his own shoes. Now he was decked out in his finery, she grinned. "Just look at you!" she said. But Diggory was solemn.

"No," he replied, "just look at you!" And he turned Martha's face into the light.

Her eye was the colour of a Thames sunset – yellow and purple and blue jostling together.

"Did he do this to you?" Diggory demanded, "Mr Poole?"

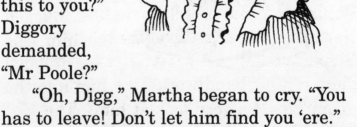

"Oh, Digg," Martha began to cry. "You has to leave! Don't let him find you 'ere."

"Too late!" William said. Behind them, a black shadow swayed against the light from the hall. Poole!

"Get out of my house!" he growled. "Get out!"

"Did you do this to her?" Diggory demanded.

"That's none of your concern," Poole lurched into the room. He had to clutch at a dresser for support. "Get out before I call the  constables. And take those ill-bred street vermin with you!"

"Call the peelers if you want to!" said William. "And we'll tell them how you treat your servants!" He pointed to Bennet's bandaged wrist. "I take it this is more of your handiwork?"

"Why you little . . ." Mr Poole loomed forward. As he pushed away from the dresser, it rocked alarmingly.

"Look out!" Diggory cried. Mr Poole

looked round groggily, but the dresser
was already toppling. Pans crashed,
crockery smashed, and when silence
returned, there was Mr Poole, lying
under everything, groaning, and gasping
for breath.

"Get . . . this thing . . . off me," he rasped. "I . . . can't . . . breathe!"

"Come on you lot!" said Diggory. But when he looked around, the mudlarks had gone. The threat of the constable must have frightened them off.

They tried, the four of them, But the dresser was huge and solid. Bennet could only use his good hand, and William wasn't used to heavy lifting. All together, they only shifted the thing half an inch.

"Please!" Poole gasped. "I'll do anything, only . . . *help me!*"

Diggory scoured the room. There must be something. Something to use. Think, Diggory, think, he told himself.

Above him the clothes drier hung from pulleys. The cords they hung from looked good and strong. And the shelf above the cooking range was pretty sturdy . . .

"Quick, give us a hand!" he said, and started issuing orders.

Within minutes, the thing was done.

The drier was down and stripped of its cords, the shelf was cleared and prised from its brackets. William and Diggory used one end of the pulley rope to lash the shelf and the chair together. Then Diggory climbed on to Bennet's shoulders to pass the free end back through the pulleys. Meanwhile Martha tied the

second cord like a sling under the dresser.

"What's the idea here then? Bennet asked as Diggory wedged one end of the shelf under the heavy cast-iron cooking range. Diggory put the finishing touches to his contraption. Then he stood back and wiped his hands on his waistcoat.

"Counterweight!" he said.

"Now Bennet," he continued, dragging the scullery table noisily to where the chair now floated, "when I say 'now' all you have to do is . . . sit down. In that chair. With your weight and us pulling, we should be able to shift this thing."

"Better do it quick, Digg," Martha cried. "Mr Poole's gone a right funny colour!"

"Right!" Diggory commanded. "William, you get ready to lift with me; Martha, you stand by to pull Mr Poole out from under. Alright everyone . . ." He looked round at the tense, expectant faces. "One . . . two . . . THREE!" Bennet leapt into the chair. The chair groaned, the plank groaned, Mr Poole groaned, but the dresser didn't shift.

"C'mon William," Diggory yelled, "Heave!!"

The two boys strained. For a moment it seemed hopeless, then, with a creak and a crack, the dresser rose a few precious inches.

"Look out!" Martha was pointing up at the pulley.

"It can't take the strain much longer!" cried Diggory, "Get him out, Martha – quick!"

Martha pulled. Mr Poole scrambled. As he dragged his legs clear, the pulley finally gave out. The dresser, the chair and Bennet all landed together with a ground-shaking crash.

"Diggory!" William said, slapping his friend on the back. "You are a genius!! Brunel couldn't have done it better!"

Poole was dusting himself down. "Bennet," he ordered, "Run and fetch a constable. Tell him I have been attacked in my own home, and my property destroyed by these . . . vandals!"

"But . . . sir . . ."

"Do it!"

"But you did that yourself!" Diggory protested. "We rescued you!"

"You? Rescue me?" Poole snarled, "A sly, devious, barely educated country ruffian. Who would believe you?"

"I would, Gerald."

The suddenness of the quiet words was more shocking than a gunshot. They all whirled round. "Mother!" Poole cried. "You shouldn't be up!"

"I heard a noise." The old lady hobbled into the room, surveyed the damage, and laid a gentle hand on Martha's bruised cheek. "My dear," she said. "I had no idea things had got so bad. Gerald was such a good man before his dear wife passed away."

"Mother," Poole stammered, "I . . ." But Mrs Poole held up her hand for silence.

"Bennet," she said, "Be so good as to order a carriage to take these children home. And then, Gerald, I wish to see you . . . in the drawing room."

In the carriage on the way home,

William turned to Diggory. "That was . . ." he began.

"I know," Diggory groaned. "I'm sorry."

" . . . Without doubt . . . "

"I said I was sorry!"

". . . The most exciting night of my life!"

"I know. I should never have dragged . . . eh?"

William grinned from ear to ear. "A chase, a rescue, a lesson in emergency engineering. I wouldn't have missed it for the world. You're a marvel, Diggory Crabtree. An absolute marvel. And I'm glad to know you."

"Blimey," said Diggory Crabtree.

8

"Well," said Mrs D'Abney sadly. "It was a
noble experiment, but I am wise enough,
I hope, to know when it has failed!"

"Failed, my dear?" said Josiah.

"But of course. Tearing across London,
bursting into private homes uninvited –
leaving the table unexcused. No truly
improved person would have behaved in
such a . . . a common manner, Josiah.
That is why I have sent Diggory home."

"Sent him home? Well – you know

best, my dear. I only hope you parted on good terms"

"Excellent terms, my dearest. He seemed particularly pleased with my parting gift."

"Parting gift?"

"I gave him that delightful sailorsuit. Why, the dear boy could hardly speak. He and William actually wept on each other's shoulders over it."

"You are sure that they were weeping, my dear?"

"Why, Josiah. What else would they have been doing?"

"What indeed, my dear? What indeed?"

A few days later, a letter arrived addressed to:

Master W. D'abney
Random Ave.
Mayfair
London W.

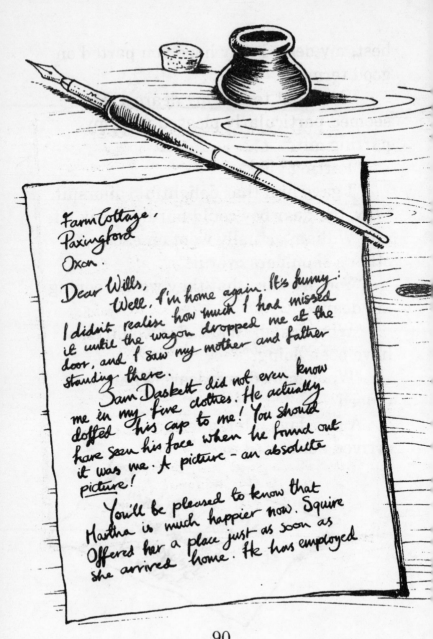

Farm Cottage,
Paxingford
Oxon.

Dear Wills,
        Well, I'm home again. It's funny:
I didn't realise how much I had missed
it until the wagon dropped me at the
door, and I saw my mother and father
standing there.
        Sam Daskett did not even know
me in my fine clothes. He actually
doffed his cap to me! You should
have seen his face when he found out
it was me. A picture — an absolute
picture!
            You'll be pleased to know that
Martha is much happier now. Squire
offered her a place just as soon as
she arrived home. He has employed

Bennet too as his personal valet, and the best news of all is that they are to be married in the summer—

Martha and Bennet, that is, not Bennet and the Squire!

I had another letter from Silas—sorry, <u>Uncle</u> Silas—today. He's found an engineering firm that are willing to take me on as an apprentice. So Mr. Brunel will need to look out Diggory Crabtree is on his way!

Do give your Ma and Pa my regards I owe them a lot. You must all come and visit the farm soon. Oh, and by the way, Wills, please tell your ma that, although I don't wear the sailor suit now, it has pride of place as the "uniform" for the fellow who took over my old job....

Your friend,

Digg

THE END

Also by Hodder Children's Books

THE CRABTREE CHRONICLES

Robin Kingsland

Book 1: LET'S GET CAESAR!

Eddie Crabtree - an ordinary kid with an ordinary life. But his ancestors were anything but ordinary. Take young Marcus Crabbius, way back in Roman times . . .

Caesar's birthday looms, and Marcus Crabbius is fed up. The great general, Gaius Agrippa, is coming to stay for the celebrations, along with his daughter - the dreadful Druisilla. What a total bore . . .
But then Marcus and Druisilla find themselves involved in a terrible conspiracy against Caesar himself - it's all a little bit too exciting . . .

Oh, for a bit of peace and quiet!

93

THE CRABTREE CHRONICLES

Robin Kingsland

Book 2: BLAME IT ON THE BARD!

Eddie Crabtree - an ordinary kid with an ordinary life. But his ancestors were anything but ordinary. Take young Perkin Crabbetrie, way back in Tudor times . . .

Perkin's passion is the theatre. He longs to see a play performed - maybe one by that Mr Shakespeare. His parents don't approve at all!

But Perkin is determined. And when he finds himself inside the new town playhouse he can hardly believe his luck!

Until what happens next makes him rather wish he'd stayed at home . . .

Also by Hodder Children's Books

THE CRABTREE CHRONICLES

Robin Kingsland

Book 5: ABSENT WITHOUT LEIF

Eddie Crabtree - an ordinary kid with an ordinary life. But his ancestors were anything but ordinary. Take young Freya Crabbtrygge, way back in Viking times . . .

Freya's a peace-loving girl at heart, but she can weild an axe better than any boy. Including her twin brother, Leif.

So when it's time for Leif to set sail and go 'a viking', Freya offers to take his place. She's not afraid to fight for her family's honour . . .

Until she sees the size of her opponent, that is!

THE CRABTREE CHRONICLES

0 340 69989 2   Book 1: Let's Get Caesar!   £3.50 ☐
0 340 69966 3   Book 2: Blame the Bard !   £3.50 ☐
0 340 72713 6   Book 5: Absent Without Leif   £3.50 ☐

All Hodder Children's books are available at your local bookshop, or can be ordered direct from the publisher. Just tick the titles you would like and complete the details below. Prices and availability are subject to change without prior notice.

Please enclose a cheque or postal order made payable to Bookpoint Ltd and send to Hodder Children's Books, 39 Miton Park, Abingdon, OXON OX14 4TD, UK. Or email at: orders@book-point.co.uk

If you would prefer to pay by credit card, our call centre team would be delighted to take your order by phone. Our direct line is 01235 400414 (9am-6pm Monday to Saturday). Alternatively you can fax on 01235 400454.

TITLE		FIRST NAME		SURNAME	
ADDRESS					
DAYTIME TEL			POSTCODE		

If you would prefer to pay by credit card, please complete:
Please debit my Visa/Access/Diner's Card/American Express
(delete as applicable).

Signature . . . . Expiry date . . . . . .